Fables You Shouldn't Pay Any Attention To

Florence Parry Heide
and Sylvia Worth Van Clief
Pictures by Victoria Chess

A Yearling Book

Published by
Dell Publishing
a division of
Bantam Doubleday Dell Publishing Group, Inc.
666 Fifth Avenue
New York, New York 10103

ISBN: 0-440-40473-8

Reprinted by arrangements with the authors and artist

Printed in the United States of America

June 1991

10 9 8 7 6 5 4 3 2 1

CWO

To Bets and Barl, remembering

the one that was, the time that was,

and the songs that will be sung.

Contents

Genevieve

Genevieve was careless.

Isn't that terrible? She was very, very careless.

All the other children took off their good clothes and put on their old play clothes when they went outside to play.

But not Genevieve. She played in her very best dresses. So all of her very best dresses were dirty and stained and torn.

All the other children were very careful
with their toys. They always put them away
when they were through playing. Their
dolls and trucks and bikes and games were
just like new. They never got lost. They
never got broken. They never got wet.
They never wore out.

But Genevieve was very, very careless with her toys. She left her bike outside to get rusty. Her doll was in terrible shape. *All* of her toys were in terrible shape. The ones that weren't broken were wet. The ones that weren't broken or wet were lost.

Oh, Genevieve was careless, all right.

When Christmastime came near, her father and mother sat down to make out a Christmas list.

"None of the children really needs a thing," said her mother. "Their clothes are just like new. Their toys are just like new. But Genevieve needs all new dresses. And Genevieve needs all new toys."

So that year the other children got very little for Christmas.

Genevieve got all new clothes and all new
toys.

"It pays to be careless," thought
Genevieve, as she rode her beautiful new
bike around the block.

Cyril

Cyril and Jennifer were squirrels.
They lived in the forest.
Cyril was very, very, very selfish.
That wasn't very nice. You're supposed
to *share*. Jennifer shared. But not Cyril.

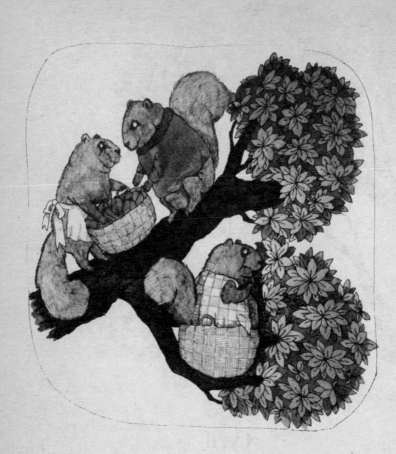

"Hey, can I have some of your nuts?" one
of the other squirrels would ask Jennifer.

"Help yourself," Jennifer would say.

"Hey, can I have some of your nuts?" one
of the other squirrels would ask Cyril.

"Drop dead," Cyril would say.

"You're selfish, Cyril," the other squirrels would say. "You're supposed to share, the way Jennifer does."

Jennifer kept giving her nuts to the other squirrels. Cyril was too selfish. He kept all of his nuts to himself.

"Hey, can I have some of your nuts, Jennifer?" asked Cyril.

"Help yourself," said Jennifer.

Winter came. Jennifer had given all of her
nuts away.

"Hey, can I have some of your nuts,
Cyril?" asked Jennifer.

"Drop dead," said Cyril.

And she did.

"I'm glad I was selfish," said Cyril. "It pays."

Muriel

All the cows were very happy at the farm. And no wonder. The farmer and his wife were kind, and the grass was very green. The cows could eat green grass all day long. Who could ask for anything more?

Muriel.

Muriel was discontented. "Look how green the grass is on the other side of the fence," Muriel said. "That farm looks nicer than this one."

"This one is nice," said the other cows, chewing the nice green grass.

"And look at that big white farmhouse over there. Its windows must be made of diamonds," said Muriel. "See how they shine."

"It's just the sun shining on the windows that makes them look like diamonds," said the other cows, happily chewing their nice green grass. "Try to be contented, Muriel," they said.

"That farmer is probably so rich he'd give me a diamond collar," said Muriel. "Anyway, that grass is certainly greener than this grass. I'm going over there."

So Muriel started off alone. All the other cows kept chewing their nice green grass and being contented.

Muriel walked and walked and walked.

She kept walking and walking and walking and finally she reached the other farm.

"Why, the grass *is* greener here," said Muriel. "It's the greenest grass in the world." And it was.

She looked at the big white farmhouse.

"And the windows *are* made of diamonds," she said. And they were.

The new farmer and his wife were very,
very kind and very, very rich. The farmer
brushed Muriel's coat every day. The farmer's wife gave Muriel a diamond collar.

"It pays to be discontented," said Muriel,
as she chewed the greenest, juiciest grass in
the world.

Gretchen

Gretchen was greedy.

All the other little fish had good manners. All the other little fish ate only what they should, and no more.

But not Gretchen. Gretchen was too greedy. She was always the first one to rush to the table at mealtime and she was always the last one to leave. She loved to eat. "It keeps my spirits up," said Gretchen.

One day Gretchen kept sitting and eating long, long after all the other little fish had excused themselves and left the table. She had five helpings of seaweed salad and seven helpings of kelp cakes.

By that time Gretchen could hardly swim. She floated around, thinking she should exercise or she wouldn't feel like having supper that night, and that would really be terrible.

While she was floating around she saw a worm on a hook. There it was, right in front of her, and it looked particularly delicious.

Now Gretchen really loved worms. More than seaweed salad, more than kelp cakes, Gretchen loved worms.

But she had eaten so much that she didn't have room for one more bite—even a bite of a worm.

"My big chance to eat a nice juicy worm," thought Gretchen sadly, "but I was too greedy at lunch."

So she swam away from the worm on the hook.

All the other little fish, who had not been as greedy as Gretchen, saw the worm on the hook. And they saw lots of other worms on other hooks.

"Oh, good!" they said. "We're glad *we're* still hungry. We're glad *we* weren't greedy at lunchtime, like Gretchen."

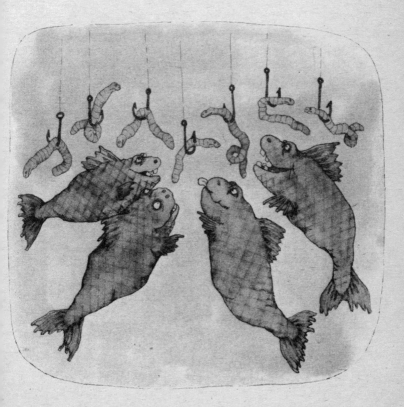

So all the other little fish were caught by fishermen that day.

That night Gretchen sat alone at the table. She ate her own dinner, and then she went around the table eating the dinners of all the other little fish.

"It pays to be greedy," sighed Gretchen
happily.

Chester

Chester was lazy.

Chester was the *laziest* turkey you ever heard of.

The other turkeys were always very busy doing whatever it is that all good turkeys should be doing.

But not Chester. He was too lazy.

He was too lazy to get out of bed.

"What would I do if I *did* get up?" he asked.

"Make your bed," said the other turkeys, who always made theirs.

"What's the use? I'm only going to get right back in it again," said Chester.

As you see, he was very lazy.

If he was inside, he was too lazy to go outside.

If he was outside, he was too lazy to go inside.

He was too lazy to go "gobble gobble."
And all turkeys go "gobble gobble."

One chilly morning the farmer called the turkeys.

"Here turkey, turkey, turkey, turkey, turkey!" called the farmer.

All the other turkeys got ready to run to the farmer to see what he wanted. ".Come on, Chester," said the other turkeys.

"I'm going to stay in bed," said Chester.

"You're so lazy, Chester. How will you know what the farmer wants?" asked the other turkeys.

"Come back and tell me," yawned Chester.

"Lazybones," said the other turkeys. They all ran to see what it was the farmer wanted.

The next morning, which was Thanks-
giving morning, Chester looked around
the empty barn. "It pays to be lazy," thought
Chester, turning over for a little nap.

Annette

All the little monkeys were just finishing breakfast when the father monkey said, "Remember, today is the day we're going to put up a nice new swing. We'll hang it from the highest tree."

"Oh, good," said all the little monkeys.

"But first we'll have to pick all of the coconuts and pile them in neat little piles," said the father monkey. "Then after we've done all of our work, we can swing and swing."

Annette sighed. "I hate to pick coconuts and pile them in neat little piles," she thought.

Then she said, "I feel sick." That was not true. "I feel terrible," she said. *That* was true. She felt terrible because she was afraid she was going to have to pick coconuts and pile them in neat little piles.

"Oh dear," said the mother monkey. "Then you'll have to go to bed, dear."

46

So Annette went to bed.

"How do you feel now, dear?" asked the mother monkey.

"Terrible," said Annette. That was not true. "I think I'd feel better if you'd read to me." *That* was true. Annette loved to have her mother read to her.

The mother monkey read to Annette. She
read seven books. "How do you feel now,
dear?" she asked Annette.

"I think I'd feel better if I had something
to eat," said Annette. That was true. Annette loved to eat.

So the mother monkey brought Annette a nice banana and some coconut milk.

"How do you feel now, dear?" asked the mother monkey.

"I think I'd feel better if I had a softer bed," said Annette. That was true.

So the mother monkey asked the father
monkey and the little monkeys to bring soft
leaves and branches to make a new bed for
Annette. Then they went back to work
picking coconuts. Annette stayed in her soft
bed.

Finally the coconuts were all picked and piled in neat little piles. Finally the swing was hung from the highest tree.

The father monkey and the little monkeys were so tired from doing all that work that they couldn't even eat their nice bananas and drink their coconut milk. They were too tired to play on the swing. They went to bed.

"How do you feel now, dear?" the mother monkey asked Annette.

"Terrible," said Annette. That was true. "I think I'd feel better if I went outside and got some fresh air."

So Annette went outside.

"It pays to know when to tell the truth,"
said Annette to herself, as she swung back
and forth on the new swing.

Caleb and Conrad

Caleb and Conrad were brothers.

Their parents had taught them to be polite and kind and thoughtful and gracious and truthful.

One day their mother spent all morning scrubbing the kitchen floor. She was a very neat and industrious person.

She called to Caleb and Conrad, who were outside making mudballs. "If anyone steps on my nice clean floor, he'll get a spanking," she called firmly. She was a very firm person.

Then she went upstairs to take a bath. She was a person who spent a lot of time in the bathtub.

Caleb and Conrad kept working on the mudballs until they had enough to last for six days. They were very thirsty.

"I'll go in and get us each a drink of water," said Caleb, who was a very kind and thoughtful person.

"Oh, don't bother, I'll get it," said Conrad.

"Oh, all right, then, you get it," said Caleb graciously. Caleb was a very gracious person.

So Conrad went into the kitchen and brought out a nice glass of cold water.

When their mother came downstairs after her bath and saw the kitchen floor, she came outside to visit with Caleb and Conrad.

"Who tracked mud all over my nice clean floor?" asked their mother.

"I did," said Conrad truthfully. "It pays to be truthful," thought Conrad.

Conrad was wrong.